The A to Z

School Joke Book

From **Algebra** to **Zero**!

Illustrated by Vasco Icuza

Kane Miller
A DIVISION OF EDC PUBLISHING

W9-DFK-229

GIGGLE!
BWAHAHA!
TEE-HEE!
HAHAHA!
HAH!
HE HE!
HA HA!
CACKLE!
CHORTLE!
LOL!

The A to Z School Joke Book

If you want to learn new jokes,
and love nothing more than being the class clown,
then this is the perfect book for you!

The A to Z School Joke Book is a hilarious
collection of over 300 school-themed one-liners.
The jokes are ordered alphabetically, so you
can chuckle your way from A to Z, or search for
a joke about your favorite subject. From amusing
art classes to a zany zero, the laughs don't stop!

The A to Z School Joke Book is all you need
to become a class-act comedian!

Q How can you guarantee you'll get straight **A**s?

A Use a ruler!

Q What do they tell people who flunk out of the astronaut **ACADEMY**?

A "The sky's the limit for you!"

Q Who invented **ALGEBRA**?

A An x-pert!

Q How does taking an **ALGEBRA CLASS** make you a better dancer?

A It gives you alga-rhythm!

Q How many letters are in the **ALPHABET**?

A 11: T-H-E A-L-P-H-A-B-E-T!

HAH!

Q Why did the student fail **ANATOMY**?

A Because the teacher was really sternum!

Q What should you **ANSWER** when a teacher asks you to use the word dandelion in a sentence?

A "The cheetah runs faster dandelion!"

Q Why were the fifth graders so tired on **APRIL** 1st?

A Because they had just finished a 31-day march!

Q What tools do we use in **ARITHMETIC**?

A Multipliers!

Q What happened when the **ART CLASS** made a car from pencils, rulers, erasers, and notebooks?

A They turned the key, but it remained stationary!

Q Why did the **ART STUDENT** stay up past bedtime?

A He didn't know when to draw the line!

HA HA!

Q How do you impress an **ART TEACHER**?

A Easel-y!

Q Why did the dog eat the student's **ASSIGNMENT**?

A Because it was a ruff draft!

Q What did the geography teacher say to the **ATLAS**?

A "I'd be lost without you!"

Q Why did the science student refuse to trust **ATOMS**?

A Because they make up everything!

Q What do you call a teacher who forgets to take **ATTENDANCE**?

A Absentminded!

Q What happens if you accidentally delete your teacher's **AUDIOBOOK**?

A You'll never hear the end of it!

Q Why did the drama student take a dictionary to the **AUDITION**?

A Because it was a play on words!

Q What did the librarian say when asked for **AUTHORS** of books on dinosaurs?

A "Try Sarah Topps!"

Q How did the librarian explain **AUTOBIOGRAPHIES**?

A "They're self-explanatory!"

LOL!

Q How many books can you put in an empty **BACKPACK**?

A One. After that, it's no longer empty!

Q Why didn't the students laugh at their PE teacher's **BADMINTON** joke?

A They didn't get the shuttle humor!

Q Why don't **BALLOONS** go to school?

A They're scared of the pop quizzes!

TEE-HEE!

Q Why do school nurses use red **BALLPOINT PENS**?

A In case they need to draw blood!

Q What **BAND** is always welcome in a classroom?

A A rubber band!

Q Where did the school **BAND DIRECTOR** go on vacation?

A The Florida Keys!

Q What animals always play **BASEBALL** at recess?

A Bats!

Q What did the school **BASEBALL TEAM** use to make a cake for the bake sale?

A Oven mitts and batter!

Q Why did the school **BASKETBALL** team love cookies so much?

A Because they could dunk them!

Q How do **BEES** get to school?

A They ride the school buzz!

Q How much did the piece of paper love the **BINDER**?

A A whole punch!

Q Why did the scuba divers fail **BIOLOGY**?

A Because they were below C level!

Q What did the **BIOLOGY TEACHER** wear to the school dance?

A Designer genes!

GIGGLE!

Q What kind of **BONES** are always in the music room?

A Trombones!

Q Who wrote the **BOOK** *When Does School Start*?

A Wendy Bellrings!

Q How was the **BOOKCASE** the tallest piece of furniture in the fourth grade classroom?

A It had the most stories!

Q Why do elephants use their trunks as **BOOKMARKS**?

A So they nose where they are in their books!

Q What happened when the school librarian threw some old **BOOKS** into the ocean?

A A title wave!

Q Why did the third grade teacher check the **BOOKSHELVES**?

A Just to see how they were holding up!

Q Why did the bat miss the school **BUS**?

A Because it hung around for too long!

CACKLE!

Q What goes *boing, boing, boing* in the **CAFETERIA**?

A Spring vegetables!

Q When are the school **CAFETERIA WORKERS** mean?

A When they batter fish, beat eggs, and whip cream!

Q What did one **CALCULATOR** say to the other calculator?

A "You can count on me!"

Q What do you call a student wizard who is good at **CALCULUS**?

A A math-e-magician!

Q What did the teacher say when his students couldn't name the **CAPITAL** of Alaska?

A "Come on, Juneau this one!"

GUFFAW!

Q Why did the students take their **CHAIRS** home?

A Because their teacher had asked them to take a seat!

Q How are **CHEERLEADERS** like pharaohs?

A They both like pyramids!

Q What did the **CHEMISTRY TEACHER** say about the school cafeteria?

A "When I go there, iodine!"

Q Why are **CHEMISTRY TEACHERS** so good at solving problems?

A Because they have all the solutions!

Q How many sides did the geometry teacher say a **CIRCLE** has?

A Two: the inside and the outside!

Q What is a snake's favorite **CLASS**?

A Hiss-tory!

Q Why didn't the **CLASS CLOWN** use hair oil before the test?

A She didn't want the answers to slip her mind!

Q Why were the hens asked to leave their morning **CLASSES**?

A Because they kept making yolks!

Q What did the dog say to his **CLASSMATE**?

A "Can I copy your homework? I ate mine!"

Q Why is the corner always the hottest part of the **CLASSROOM**?

A Because it's 90 degrees!

CHORTLE!

C

Q What do you call a Sasquatch who makes a wand out of **CLAY** in art class?

A Hairy Potter!

SNICKER!

Q Why do teachers keep **CLOCKS** under their desks?

A Because they're always working overtime!

Q What did the teaching assistant say when he jumped out of a storage **CLOSET**?

A "Supplies!"

Q How did the dog eat the **CODING** homework?

A In a couple of bytes!

Q Why didn't the sun go to **COLLEGE**?

A Because it already had a million degrees!

C

Q Why did the school show-off always carry a **COLORED PENCIL**?

A To draw attention!

Q What's the difference between a cat and a **COMMA**?

A One has claws at the end of its paws, and the other is a pause at the end of a clause!

Q What did the **COMPOSITION BOOK** say to the pencil?

A "Write on!"

Q Why did the teacher take the **COMPUTER** to the doctor?

A Because it had a virus!

Q Why did the **COMPUTER SCIENCE** teacher buy new glasses?

A To improve her web-sight!

CHUCKLE!

C

Q What did the PE teacher say was the fastest **COUNTRY** in the world?

A "Russia!"

GIGGLE!

Q How did students in ancient Rome do arts and **CRAFTS**?

A With Caesars and glue sticks!

Q Where did the art teacher's **CRAYONS** go on vacation?

A Colorado!

Q Why did the **CROSS-COUNTRY** team run beside the ocean?

A For the en-dolphins!

Q When do teachers go **CROSS-EYED**?

A When they can't control their pupils!

Q Why were the **DANCE** students late to class?

A They were wearing leotard-ies!

Q Who wrote the book *Teaching High School* ***DANCE CLASS***?

A Cory O'Graphy!

Q What did the history teacher say about the **DARK AGES**?

A "There were a lot of knights!"

Q What did the student say when he learned about the **DEAD SEA**?

A "I didn't even know it was sick!"

CHORTLE!

Q Why is learning about **DECIMALS** so hard?

A It can get pretty tenths!

D

Q Where did the history teacher say the **DECLARATION OF INDEPENDENCE** was signed?

A "At the bottom!"

Q Did you hear about the **DEER** who took the quiz?

A He did so well, the teacher passed the buck!

Q What did the 90-**DEGREE** angle say to the 30-degree angle in geometry class?

A "I'm always right!"

Q What did **DELAWARE** to the school dance?

A Her New Jersey!

Q Why did the snake get **DETENTION**?

A Because it was HISS-pering in class!

HAW-HAW!

Q What happened when the school's new **DICTIONARIES** were stolen?

A Everyone was at a loss for words!

Q Why is a school **DICTIONARY** dangerous?

A Because it has dynamite in it!

Q Why don't some teachers **DISPLAY** their students' drawings?

A The can make a classroom look sketchy!

Q Why don't gymnasts do well in **DRAMA CLASS**?

A They normally perform nonspeaking rolls!

Q Why does the **DRAMA TEACHER** say "break a leg" before every performance?

A Because every play needs a cast!

GUFFAW!

E

Q Which is the most **EDUCATED** dinosaur?

A The thesaurus!

Q Where do surfers go to get an **EDUCATION**?

A Boarding school!

Q What did the physics teacher say when the class reported a lost **ELECTRON**?

A "Are you positive?"

Q Why don't you see giraffes in **ELEMENTARY SCHOOL**?

A They're all in high school!

Q How often do science teachers tell jokes about the **ELEMENTS**?

A Periodically!

HA HA!

E

Q How is a flock of geese like an airplane full of **ENCYCLOPEDIAS**?

A They're both flying information!

Q Why did the history teacher tell the class that **ENGLAND** was the wettest country?

A Because the royal family has reigned there for centuries!

Q What did the students say when the **ENGLISH TEACHER** asked them to use "whom" in a sentence?

A "Can we go whom, please?"

Q What do **ENGLISH TEACHERS** eat for breakfast?

A Synonym rolls!

Q How does a pig write an **ESSAY**?

A With pen and oink!

BWAHAHA!

Q Did you hear about the fireworks **EXAM**?

A The students passed with flying colors!

Q What kind of **EXAMS** do vampire teachers give?

A Blood tests!

Q What **EXERCISES** do frogs usually do in PE class?

A Jumping jacks!

Q What did the farmer's children use for their science **EXPERIMENT**?

A A peach-tree dish!

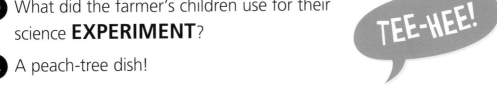

TEE-HEE!

Q Why did the music teacher have her **EYESIGHT** tested?

A She wanted to C-sharp!

Q What sort of **FACTS** do both history and art teachers love?

A Artifacts!

Q Why did the teacher call his **FIRST GRADERS** "wonder kids"?

A Because he wondered whether they'd ever learn anything!

Q How do little **FISH** get to school?

A On the octo-bus!

Q What do school librarians take with them when they go **FISHING**?

A Bookworms!

Q How is "two plus two equals **FIVE**" like your left foot?

A Because neither are right!

CACKLE!

Q What did the school **FLAGPOLE** say to the flag on its birthday?

A "I hope you have a flappy birthday!"

Q Did you hear the teachers arguing about the **FLOOD** in the cafeteria?

A Everything is OK now; it's all water under the fridge!

Q Where is the best place to grow **FLOWERS** in a school?

A In the kindergarten!

Q What happened when there was a **FOOD FIGHT** in the cafeteria?

A The food won!

HAH!

Q Why did the two number **FOURS** skip lunch period?

A They already eight!

F

Q Why did the **FOX** enroll in college after he finished school?

A To further his studies!

Q Who did the history teacher say invented **FRACTIONS**?

A Henry the Eighth!

Q What do you call a **FRIENDLY** school?

A A hi school!

Q What do **FROGS** always play at recess?

A Hopscotch!

HA HA!

Q What's the longest piece of **FURNITURE** in a school?

A The multiplication table!

Q Did you hear about the student who couldn't put the top back on her **GEL PEN**?

A She tried for hours until it suddenly clicked!

Q How do mountains make **GEOGRAPHY STUDENTS** laugh?

A They're hill-areas!

Q What's a **GEOGRAPHY TEACHER'S** favorite nation?

A Explanation!

Q What did the **GEOMETRY TEACHER** eat at lunchtime?

A A square meal!

Q Why did Diana wear **GLASSES** to math class?

A To improve her Di-vision!

LOL!

Q Who did the math teacher say was the first person to travel around the **GLOBE**?

A Sir Cumference!

LOL!

Q Why did the teacher cover her textbooks in **GLUE**?

A So her students couldn't put them down!

Q What did the **GLUE STICK** say to the art teacher?

A "I'm stuck on you!"

Q What is the first thing that a **GORILLA** learns in school?

A The ape-BCs!

Q What do you call a nut that gets good **GRADES**?

A An academia nut!

Q What kind of school makes you drop out before you can **GRADUATE**?

A Skydiving school!

Q What do you say to comfort someone struggling with **GRAMMAR**?

A "There, their, they're!"

Q Why don't teachers trust students who use **GRAPH PAPER**?

A They're always plotting something!

Q Why was the math teacher disappointed by the film about **GRAPHS**?

A The plot was predictable, and the special f(x) were terrible!

Q What is the center of **GRAVITY**?

A The letter *V*!

SNICKER!

Q How did the thief steal all the **HAND** sanitizer from the school?

A By making a clean getaway!

Q Why do teachers always want you to practice your **HANDWRITING**?

A Because it's the write thing to do!

Q Did you hear about the science teacher that gave the class books on **HELIUM**?

A No one could put them down!

Q Which state is round at each end and **HIGH** in the middle?

A Ohio!

Q What did the teacher say when he couldn't find his **HIGHLIGHTER**?

A "I guess it's a bye-lighter now!"

HAHAHA!

Q Who did the social studies teacher say was the biggest thief in **HISTORY**?

A Atlas—he held up the whole world!

Q What do **HISTORY STUDENTS** talk about at parties?

A The good old days!

Q What do **HISTORY TEACHERS** call it when they get together?

A A date!

Q Where do the school's **HOCKEY COACHES** do their paperwork?

A At the office!

Q Which animal did the students want as their school **HOCKEY TEAM** mascot?

A The score-pion!

GIGGLE!

Q How is slippery sidewalk **ICE** like music class?

A Because if you don't C-sharp, you'll B-flat!

Q How come the king of the classroom is only 12 **INCHES** tall?

A Because he's a ruler!

Q What did the fifth grader get when she divided the circumference of a **JACK-O-LANTERN** by its diameter?

A Pumpkin pi!

Q Why did the teacher marry the school **JANITOR**?

A Because he swept her off her feet!

Q What's the difference between a PE student **JOGGING** and a dog running?

A One wears shorts, and the other pants!

HE HE!

Q What happened when the computer teacher's laptop was missing a **KEY**?

A She lost ctrl!

Q Why did the music teacher keep banging his head on the **KEYBOARD**?

A He was playing by ear!

Q What flies around the **KINDERGARTEN** classroom at nighttime?

A The alpha-bat!

Q Which medieval **KING** wrote the school librarian's favorite books?

A King Author!

Q How do **KNIGHTS** communicate in computer class?

A By chain mail!

HA HA!

L

Q Why did the fifth graders put a **LADDER** in their classroom?

A They wanted to go to high school!

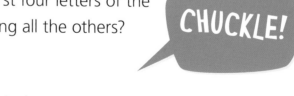

Q What happened when the Spanish **LANGUAGE** club went on a cruise?

A They got lost at sí!

Q Why was the teacher's **LAPTOP** late for school?

A It had a hard drive!

Q Why should the teacher **LEARN** not to be mad at his lazy students?

A Because they didn't do anything!

Q Why is **LEARNING** the first four letters of the alphabet harder than learning all the others?

A The rest is just E–Z!

CHUCKLE!

L

Q What has 18 **LEGS** and catches flies?

A The school baseball team!

Q What is the first thing to do in a yodeling **LESSON**?

A Form an orderly, orderly, orderly line!

Q What color is the **LETTER** *M*?

A Pastel!

HAH!

Q Which word of five **LETTERS** has six left when you take two away?

A Sixty!

Q Why did the school **LIBRARIAN** buy 7,654 new books?

A No shelf-control!

Q Why was the clock in the school **LIBRARY** muffled?

A Because there is no tocking in the library!

Q Where do **LIONS** go to school?

A Maine!

Q When is a bad school **LUNCH** like a history lesson?

A When you delve into ancient grease!

Q What stops a **LUNCHROOM** food fight?

A A peas treaty!

HAHAHA!

Q What did one cafeteria tray say to the other at **LUNCHTIME**?

A "Lunch is on me!"

Q What did the geography teacher say when she found her missing **MAPS**?

A "Atlas!"

Q What happened when the **MARCHING** band dropped all their instruments?

A It was band-emonium!

Q Why can't you have **MATH CLASS** in the jungle?

A Because if you add 4 and 4 you get ate!

Q What's a **MATH TEACHER'S** favorite winter sport?

A Figure skating!

Q Why did the cell cross the **MICROSCOPE** in the science lab?

A To get to the other slide!

TEE-HEE!

Q Are **MONSTERS** good at math tests?

A Not unless you Count Dracula!

Q Where do kids in New York City learn their **MULTIPLICATION** tables?

A Times Square!

Q What happened when the **MUSIC ROOM** was burgled?

A The burglars ran off with the lute!

Q Why couldn't the **MUSIC TEACHER** open the classroom?

A Because the keys were on the piano!

Q What **MUSICAL INSTRUMENT** does the band director keep in her bathroom?

A A tuba toothpaste!

CACKLE!

Q Did you hear about the math teacher who was afraid of **NEGATIVE NUMBERS**?

A He stops at nothing to avoid them!

Q Why did the student want to go to **NIGHT SCHOOL**?

A To learn to read in the dark!

Q What does the teacher say about **NOTEBOOKS** with perforated pages?

A "They're tear-able!"

Q What do you call a **NUMBER** that can't keep still?

A A roamin' numeral!

BWAHAHA!

Q Why did Dracula's son get sent to the school **NURSE**?

A Because he was coffin!

Q Do you know what seems **ODD** to math teachers?

A Numbers that can't be divided by two!

Q How do food science teachers teach their students to make **OMELETS**?

A By eggs-ample!

Q How did the math teacher make **ONE** vanish?

A By adding *g* to make it gone!

Q Why are spiders so good at **ONLINE** learning?

A They are already comfortable on the web!

Q What did the **OWL** say when the teacher caught it talking in class?

A "I'm talon you, it wasn't me!"

HAW-HAW!

Q How are some teachers' jokes like **PAPER**?

A They fall flat!

SNICKER!

Q How do **PCs** learn new things in class?

A Bit by bit!

Q What should you do if your **PEN** runs out?

A Chase after it!

Q Would you like to hear a joke about a blunt **PENCIL**?

A There's no point!

Q Have you heard about the **PENS** that can write underwater?

A They can write lots of other words, too!

Q What do you call a **PENCIL SHARPENER** that can't sharpen pencils?

A Broken!

Q Where do all classroom **PENCILS** come from?

A Pennsylvania!

HE HE!

Q If the **PILGRIMS** arrived on the *Mayflower*, what did the teachers travel on?

A Scholarships!

Q What happened to the **PLANT** in the math room?

A It grew square roots!

Q What did the drama students do when they made a mistake during the **PLAY**?

A They reacted!

Q Why did the student cross the **PLAYGROUND**?

A To get to the other slide!

Q Where do **POEMS** come from?

A Poe-trees!

Q How do **POETS** greet each other on the first day of class?

A "Haven't we metaphor?"

Q What does the school's champion **POLE VAULTER** drink?

A Spring water!

Q What did the **POLYGON** say when the circle asked how to be edgier?

A "Triangles!"

Q Who wrote the book *Outside the **PRINCIPAL'S** Office*?

A Watts E. Dunn!

Q What is the answer to the algebra **PROBLEM**, 5Q + 5Q?

A 10Q … and you're welcome!

Q Have you heard about the frog **PROFESSORS**?

A They give ribbit-ing lectures!

Q What should you say when your teacher gives you a B+ on your sewing **PROJECT**?

A "Seams reasonable!"

CHORTLE!

Q Who did Frankenstein's monster take to the **PROM**?

A His ghoul-friend!

44

Q What should you say if your teacher asks you to name two **PRONOUNS**?

A "Who, me?"

LOL!

Q What do you call a disagreeable **PROTRACTOR**?

A A contractor!

Q Why do words and **PUNCTUATION** always end up in court?

A To be sentenced!

Q What do you call a teacher with just one **PUPIL**?

A Cyclops!

Q Why did the students put **PUSHPINS** on their shirts?

A They wanted to look sharp!

Q Why do **QUARTERBACKS** always take the hardest classes?

A Because they know they can pass!

Q What do you call an elderly teacher that asks a lot of **QUESTIONS**?

A Pop quiz!

BWAHAHA!

Q Did you hear about the **QUIZ** in cooking class?

A It was a piece of cake!

Q What do students do at recess on **RAINY DAYS**?

A They play bored games!

Q What books do planets like to **READ** during library time?

A Comet books!

Q What is a history teacher's favorite **ROCK** group?

A Mount Rushmore!

Q Who enjoys learning about **ROMAN NUMERALS** in math class?

A I for one!

HAH!

Q Which **ROOM** can a student never enter?

A A mushroom!

Q Where can you buy a **RULER** that is three feet long?

A At a yard sale!

Q Why did the students **RUN** out of the classroom?

A They were being chased by a spelling bee!

Q Who should be your best friend at **SCHOOL**?

A The principal!

Q Which **SCHOOL BUILDING** has the most stories?

A The library!

Q What type of **SCHOOL BUS** can't you ride on?

A The syllabus!

Q Why was the clock in the **SCHOOL CAFETERIA** slow?

A It always went back four seconds!

Q What do you grow in an elementary **SCHOOL GARDEN**?

A Human beans!

GUFFAW!

Q Where did the **SCHOOL LIBRARIAN** fall asleep?

A Between the covers!

Q What color are the books in the **SCHOOL LIBRARY**?

A They are all red!

Q What happened when thieves walked onstage during the **SCHOOL PLAY**?

A They stole the spotlight!

Q Why did the **SCHOOLHOUSE** go to see the doctor?

A It had windowpanes!

Q How do **SCHOOLYARD** trees access the internet?

A They log on!

Q What do you say to a **SCIENCE TEACHER** whose classroom smells like eggs?

A "Sorry for your sulfuring!"

Q Why did the preschool teacher want a new pair of **SCISSORS**?

A The old ones just weren't cutting it anymore!

Q What do you get when you graduate from **SCUBA DIVING** school?

A A deep-loma!

Q What's a math teacher's favorite **SEASON**?

A Summer!

TEE-HEE!

Q Why did the **SECOND GRADER** study on an airplane?

A To get higher grades!

Q How do you make **SEVEN** an even number?

A Take out the *S*!

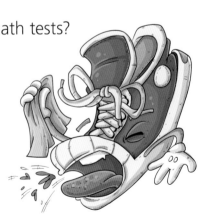

CACKLE!

Q What has forty feet and **SINGS**?

A The school choir!

Q What did the **SIXTH GRADERS** do when their shoelaces got tangled together?

A They went on a class trip!

Q What kind of **SNAKES** do the best on math tests?

A Adders!

Q What did the **SNEAKER** say when it sneezed during PE?

A "A shoe!"

S

Q Why do **SOCCER** players do so well in school?

A They know how to use their heads!

Q Why was the after-school **SOCCER CLUB** all dressed up?

A They were going to the soccer ball!

Q Do you want to hear the chemistry teacher's **SODIUM** joke?

A Na!

Q Which superhero was the star of their school **SOFTBALL** team?

A Batgirl!

Q What's the difference between a student who doesn't understand figures of **SPEECH** and a burglar?

A The first takes things literally. The other takes things, literally!

Q How did the chemistry teacher **SPELL** hard water with three letters?

A ICE!

Q Why shouldn't you try **SPELLING** the word "part" backward?

A It's a trap!

Q What do you get when you cross a pebble with a **SPHERE** in geometry class?

CACKLE!

A Rock and roll!

Q Which **SPORT** is always in trouble at school?

A Badminton!

Q What did the **SQUARE** say to the circle on the first day of school?

A "Haven't I seen you around?"

Q Did you hear about the music teachers who made a band**STAND**?

A She took away their chairs!

Q Why can't **STAPLERS** leave the classroom?

A Because they are stationery!

Q Which **STATE** did the best at school?

A Alabama, with four As and one B!

Q Did you hear the joke about the school **STATISTICIAN**?

A Probably!

Q How did the beauty school **STUDENT** do on her manicure test?

A She nailed it!

GIGGLE!

Q Where did King Arthur **STUDY**?

A Knight school!

Q What's a witch's favorite **SUBJECT**?

A Spelling!

Q Why does the school **SWIM TEAM** set up their phones to update before they get in the pool?

A So, they can sync and swim at the same time!

Q What did the PE teacher say to the impatient **SWIMMER**?

A "Whoa, whoa, whoa … wade just a minute!"

Q What type of stroke did the music teacher do in the **SWIMMING POOL**?

A The Bach stroke!

HAHAHA!

Q What **TABLES** do you *not* have to learn in second-grade math?

A Lunch tables!

Q Why did the teacher send the computer **TABLET** to the dentist?

A Because it had Bluetooth!

HAHAHA!

Q What did the mean triangle whisper to the **TAMBOURINE** during math class?

A "You're pointless!"

Q Which subject did the butterfly **TEACH** at insect school?

A Moth-ematics!

Q What did the ghost **TEACHER** say to the class?

A "Look at the board, and I'll go through it again!"

Q When do **TEACHERS** wear sunglasses?

A When their students are too bright!

Q What are the **TEN** things math teachers can always count on?

A Their fingers!

Q Why don't PE teachers like being on the **TENNIS COURT**?

A They can't stand all the racket!

Q Why did the hungry PE students glue coins to their **TENNIS SHOES**?

A To get cashews!

LOL!

Q What kinds of **TESTS** do witches do best on?

A Hex-aminations and spelling bees!

Q What did the frog say when he picked up the **TEXTBOOK**?

A "Read it, read it, read it!"

Q Why did the students use the school **THEATER'S** trapdoor?

A They were going through a stage!

Q Did you hear about the world's worst **THESAURUS**?

A Not only is it awful, it's awful!

Q What type of **TREES** do math teachers climb?

A Geome-trees!

HA HA!

Q What do you call a **TRIANGLE** that gets into an accident?

A A wrecked-angle!

Q Why was the **TRIGONOMETRY** class confusing?

A The teacher went off on a tangent!

Q Why did the bee get into **TROUBLE** at school?

A Because he wasn't bee-hiving very well!

Q How did the music teacher fix the broken **TUBA**?

A With a tube-a glue!

Q What book is about an onion that **TURNS** into a spider?

A *Shallot's Web*!

Q What font do mermaids use when they're **TYPING** book reports?

A Ariel!

CHORTLE!

Q Did you hear about the **UNDERWATER** school choir?

A They sing aqua-pella!

Q What **UNIT** of measurement do you use in biology class to weigh bones?

A Skeletons!

HE HE!

Q What did the math teacher say is bigger when it's **UPSIDE** down?

A The number 6!

Q What did the **US FLAG** say to the Canadian flag?

A Nothing! It just waved!

Q What **US STATE** has the most math teachers?

A Math-achussetts!

V

Q Why don't **VAMPIRES** have any friends at school?

A Because they're a pain in the neck!

Q How did the history student say **VIKINGS** sent secret messages to each other?

A "By Norse code!"

Q How does a **VIOLA** greet a music teacher?

A "Cello!"

Q What did the geology teacher say to the **VOLCANO**?

A "I lava you!"

Q Why did the school **VOLLEYBALL COACH** bring extra shoelaces to the court?

A To tie the score!

LOL!

Q What answer did the student give to the geography quiz question, "What is the capital of **WASHINGTON**?"

A "W!"

Q Why did the art teacher take **WAX CRAYONS** home at night?

A In order to draw the curtains!

Q Why did the teacher write on the **WINDOW**?

A To make sure the lesson was clear!

Q What did the music teacher call the big-footed **WOODWIND** player?

A A Sax-quatch!

Q What type of spelling **WORDS** have two *u*'s?

A I don't know, but they must be unique!

BWAHAHA!

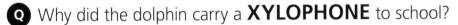

Q Why did the dolphin carry a **XYLOPHONE** to school?

A It was in the orca-stra!

Q What did the math teacher say to the **YARDSTICK**?

A "You rule!"

Q What should you answer when your teacher asks, "How many seconds are there in a **YEAR**?"

A "Twelve! January 2nd, February 2nd, March 2nd …"

Q Did you hear that the school hockey team reported their **ZAMBONI** driver missing?

A Let's hope he resurfaces soon!

HAHAHA!

Q What did all the teachers do when one student got a **ZERO** in every subject?

A They made a lot of fuss about nothing!

LOL!

CACKLE!

HE HE!

BWAHAHA!

HA HA!

First American Edition 2021
Kane Miller, A Division of EDC Publishing
Copyright © Green Android Ltd 2021
Illustrated by Vasco Icuza

For information contact:
Kane Miller, A Division of EDC Publishing
5402 S 122nd E Ave
Tulsa, OK 74146
www.kanemiller.com
www.myubam.com

All rights reserved. No part of this publication may be reproduced, stored in a retrieval system, or transmitted in any form or by any means, electronic, mechanical, photocopying, recording or otherwise without the prior written permission of the publisher.

Library of Congress Control Number: 2021930485

Printed and bound in Malaysia, July 2021
ISBN: 978-1-68464-325-7